Hyperion Chapters

The Peanut Butter Gang
Catherine Siracusa

Hyperion Books for Children
New York

To my cousin,
Leo Politi

Text and illustrations © 1996 by Catherine Siracusa.
All rights reserved.
For information address Hyperion Books for Children,
114 Fifth Avenue, New York, New York 10011-5690.
Printed in the United States of America.
First Edition
1 3 5 7 9 10 8 6 4 2
The artwork for each picture is prepared using pencil, watercolor, and gouache.
This book is set in 19-point Goudy.

Library of Congress Cataloging-in-Publication Data
Siracusa, Catherine
The peanut butter gang / [text and illustrations] by Catherine
Siracusa.—1st ed.
p. cm.
Summary: Billy Hardy must outwit a gang of squirrels to save Mr.
Dingsley and his doorbell factory.
ISBN 0-7868-0148-4 (trade)—ISBN 0-7868-1115-3 (pbk.)
[1. Bells—Fiction. 2. Peanut butter—Fiction. 3. Rabbits—
Fiction. 4. Squirrels—Fiction] I. Title.
PZ7.S6215Pe 1996
[E]—dc 20   95-21937

Contents

Chapter One
Billy Hardy

In the town of Bellville, the Dingdong Doorbell Factory was a very noisy place. Doorbells rang all day long. *Dingdong! Dingdong! Dingdong!*

It was so loud, everyone wore earmuffs. But not Billy Hardy, the chief doorbell ringer.

"I love bells," he said. "I love the ringing and the dinging, the ding and the dong of doorbells ringing."

Billy came from a family of bell

ringers. His mother rang the bell
on a train. His father rang the
bell on an ice-cream truck. His
grandmother rang the bell on a
tugboat. His grandfather rang the
bells in an orchestra. There was
even a great-great-great-uncle, way,
way back, who rang the Liberty
Bell once or twice.

Billy had to ring all the doorbells

PHILADA
MDCCLIII

before they left the factory. He
could always tell a good doorbell
from a bad doorbell. A good
doorbell had just the right ring.
Dingdong! Dingdong! A bad doorbell
had a different ring. *Dongdunk!*
Dinkdang!

Sometimes Billy would wire up

3

ten doorbells and ring them all at the same time. Even then he could tell the difference between a good doorbell and a bad one.

"Billy, you are the best bell ringer," said his boss, Mr. Dingsley.

"Thank you, sir," said Billy.

"What?" shouted Mr. Dingsley. He took off his earmuffs.

"Thank you, sir!" shouted Billy.

"Keep up the good work," said
Mr. Dingsley. He put his earmuffs
back on.

Everyone wanted a Dingdong
Doorbell. Every day, all over
town, you could hear *dingdong!*
Dingdong!

"Bellville is a real doorbell town,"
said Mr. Dingsley.

But one day, Mr. Dingsley got some letters from unhappy customers. One letter said, "I always had a Dingdong Doorbell, but I can't stand my new one. It sounds awful!"

Another letter said, "There is something wrong with my Dingdong Doorbell. It sounds like a bad dream. No one will come to my door anymore."

And another letter said, "I am through with Dingdong Doorbells.

"Thank you, sir!" shouted Billy.

"Keep up the good work," said Mr. Dingsley. He put his earmuffs back on.

Everyone wanted a Dingdong Doorbell. Every day, all over town, you could hear *dingdong! Dingdong!*

"Bellville is a real doorbell town," said Mr. Dingsley.

But one day, Mr. Dingsley got some letters from unhappy customers. One letter said, "I always had a Dingdong Doorbell, but I can't stand my new one. It sounds awful!"

Another letter said, "There is something wrong with my Dingdong Doorbell. It sounds like a bad dream. No one will come to my door anymore."

And another letter said, "I am through with Dingdong Doorbells.

Cancel my order! I got a door knocker instead!"

"Billy, are you sending out bad doorbells?" asked Mr. Dingsley.

"No, sir," said Billy. "The bad bells never leave the factory."

"I wonder what's happening," said Mr. Dingsley.

Billy rang all the good doorbells, just to make sure they were good. *Dingdong! Dingdong! Dingdong!*

"They sound great to me," said Mr. Dingsley.

"Don't worry," said Billy. "I will deliver these good doorbells myself."

"I don't think anyone wants Dingdong Doorbells anymore," said Mr. Dingsley.

"Sure they do," said Billy. "You'll see!"

Billy put the box of good doorbells on the back of his bike. But as he rode through town, he didn't hear *dingdong! Dingdong! Dingdong!* He just heard *knock! Knock! Knock!*

"I guess Bellville is not a doorbell town anymore," said Billy sadly.

Chapter Two
Doorbell Trouble

When Billy got home, he tested his own doorbell. *Dingdong! Dingdong!*

"I love bells," said Billy. "I would never get a door knocker."

Billy went into his house. There were bells everywhere: jingle bells, dinner bells, cowbells, all kinds of bells. There was even a big painting of the Liberty Bell over his fireplace.

Billy sat in his favorite chair. "I just don't understand it," he said. "How could a good bell turn into a bad bell?"

Just then his doorbell rang. But it
didn't go *dingdong!* It went
donkdunk! Doi-oingdunk!

"Oh no," cried Billy. "Now my
doorbell sounds bad, too."

12

He ran and opened his front door.
"Hello there," said a short red
squirrel. "Having doorbell trouble?"
"I'm sure I can fix it," said Billy.

"Why bother?" asked the squirrel.
"Wouldn't you rather have one of
these?" He opened a large suitcase
filled with shiny brass door knockers.

"But I love bells," said Billy.

"All that dinging and donging?" said the squirrel. "Nothing is better than a knock."

"Not to me," said Billy. "I am the chief bell ringer at the Dingdong Doorbell Factory."

"I am Conrad Knockington. Here is my card," said the squirrel. "Give me a call if you change your mind."

Billy read the card. It said:

Knockington Door Knockers, Inc.
A knock is better than a ring!
Conrad Knockington, Vice President

"I won't change my mind," said Billy.

"We'll see about that," said Conrad. "By the way, is that Mr. Dingsley's house up on the hill?"

"Yes," said Billy. "But Mr. Dingsley would never want a door knocker."

"We'll see about that, too," said Conrad.

Conrad turned and walked to a big old car. "Let's go, gang!" he said to the two big gray squirrels in the car. "We have a pickup tonight!"

"Yeah! A pickup!" said the gray squirrels.

The car sped off.

"I'm sure I can fix my doorbell,"
said Billy. He got a screwdriver and
opened it up.

"There's peanut butter in here!"
cried Billy. "Where did it come
from?"

Then Billy found an empty jar in his flower bed. The label on the jar said:

Ma Knockington's Peanut Butter
The Stickiest, the Gooiest, the Nuttiest!

"Knockington!" said Billy. "I thought there was something nutty about Conrad Knockington. I'd better warn Mr. Dingsley!"

Chapter Three
Big Bad Squirrels

Billy jumped on his bike and rode up the hill to Mr. Dingsley's house. But he was too late. He saw Conrad and the two big gray squirrels push Mr. Dingsley into their car and drive away!

"They kidnapped Mr. Dingsley!"
cried Billy. "I have to save him!"

Billy followed the car. He saw
Conrad drive inside a big old barn.
Billy hid his bike behind some hay.
Then he tiptoed to the open barn
door and peeked inside.

21

The barn was filled with bags of peanuts, empty jars, jars filled with peanut butter, and hundreds of brass door knockers. Billy saw the two gray squirrels tie Mr. Dingsley to a chair while Conrad ate peanut butter out of a jar with a spoon.

"Poor Mr. Dingsley!" whispered Billy.

"You will never get away with this!" cried Mr. Dingsley.

"Pipe down!" said an angry voice. "I'm trying to make peanut butter up here!"

"Shh, Dingsley," said Conrad. "You're bothering Ma!"

"Shh," said the gray squirrels.

Billy was very, very quiet. He looked up and saw a fat red squirrel in the hayloft. She was turning the crank of a big nut grinder. Peanut butter oozed into a huge wooden tub on the barn floor.

That must be Ma Knockington! thought Billy.

"Ma!" said Conrad. "I got Dingsley!"

Ma climbed down from the hayloft. "Good work, Conrad," said Ma.

"What do you have against doorbells?" asked Mr. Dingsley.

"I hate bells!" said Ma. "Bells give me a headache. Bells drive me crazy!"

"Me, too!" said Conrad.

"Us, too!" said the gray squirrels.

"Besides, the peanut butter business is slow," said Ma.

"It's a real grind," said Conrad.

"I had to find something to do with all this peanut butter," said Ma.

"It can mess up any bell," said Conrad.

"Mess it up good!" said the gray squirrels.

"I plan to get rid of all the doorbells in Bellville—and all the other bells, too!" said Ma.

"No more bells?" cried Billy.

"Who said that?" asked Ma.

"I'll go and see," said Conrad.

Conrad went outside and looked around. Billy ran and hid behind a

haystack so Conrad wouldn't see
him.

"There's no one out here, Ma!"
cried Conrad. He went back inside
the barn.

"What do you want from me?" asked Mr. Dingsley.

"Our door knockers are selling well," said Ma. "But we need more room. We want to move into the Dingdong Doorbell Factory."

"It's very quiet there now," said Conrad.

"Real quiet," said the gray squirels.

"Just sign this paper, Dingsley," said Ma. "Maybe we'll give you a job at the new Knockington Door Knocker Factory."

"Never!" cried Mr. Dingsley. "I will never give my doorbell factory to you!"

"Maybe you want to take a bath in a big tub of peanut butter," said Ma.

"No!" cried Mr. Dingsley.

"Think about it," said Conrad.

"Think hard," said the gray squirrels.

Chapter Four
Saved by the Bells

Billy waited behind the haystack. I have to save Mr. Dingsley, he thought. But what can I do? I'm outnumbered!

Then Billy looked to where his bike was hidden. I've got it! he thought. The doorbells! The box of doorbells was still on the back of his bike.

Billy quickly wired up the

doorbells to the battery of his bike
light. This will drive them crazy, he
thought.

Billy got back on his bike. He
pedaled very hard and zoomed into
the barn. Then he pushed a button.
All the doorbells began to ring.
Dingdong! Dingdong! Dingdong!

The doorbells rang over and over, dinging and donging very, very loud.

"Stop those bells!" cried Ma.

"Oh, my ears!" cried Conrad.

"Help!" cried the gray squirrels.

Billy chased them around the barn.
"The noise is driving me crazy!"
cried Ma. "Let's get out of here,
boys!" Ma and her gang got into the
car. Billy rang the doorbells faster.
Dingdongdingdongdingdongdingdong!

"I can't stand it," cried Ma. She started the car but went into reverse by mistake.

Crash!

The car backed up into the huge tub of peanut butter. Sticky, gooey peanut butter oozed all over the car.

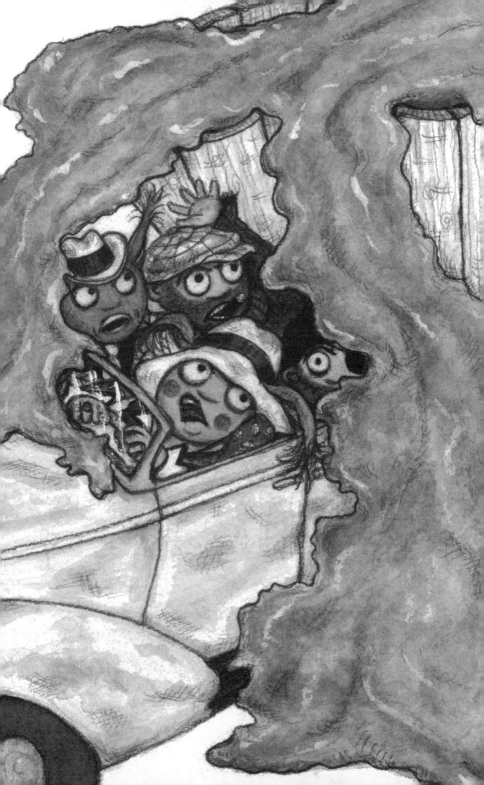

"Now we're in a real jam!" cried
Conrad.

"Help!" cried the gray squirrels.
"We're stuck!"

"Ah, nuts," said Ma. "Let's get
out of here!"

But she could not start the car.
She could not even move! The
whole gang was stuck in their
own peanut butter.

Billy got off his bike. The
doorbells were quiet.

"Good work, Billy," said Mr.
Dingsley. "Saved by the bells."

Billy untied Mr. Dingsley. "I hope
you are okay, sir," he said.

"I'm fine, thanks to you, Billy,"
said Mr. Dingsley.

Then they heard sirens. Two
police cars drove into the barn.
"What's going on?" asked the
chief of police. "We heard a lot of
bells. It sounded like a burglary."

"Oh no! The cops!" cried Ma.
"It's the Peanut Butter Gang!"
said the chief. "We've been looking
for Ma Knockington and her boys
for a long time. They stole a
truckload of peanuts last month."

The policemen got Ma, Conrad,
and the two gray squirrels out of
the car. It was not easy to do.

"What a mess!" said the chief.
"Billy, you're a hero. The Peanut
Butter Gang is going to jail!"

The next day there was a big crowd at the Dingdong Doorbell Factory. Everyone wanted to see Billy the hero. And everyone wanted a Dingdong Doorbell, because their Knockington Door Knockers were falling apart.

"Billy, you saved me and the Dingdong Doorbell Factory and all the bells in the world," said Mr. Dingsley. "I have a reward for you."

He handed Billy an envelope. Inside was a round-trip ticket to Philadelphia.

"Thank you, Mr. Dingsley!" said Billy. "I'm going to see the Liberty Bell!"

The crowd cheered, "Hooray for
Billy Hardy!" Billy was so happy
that he rang all the bells in the
factory at once. *Dingdong! Dingdong!
Dingdong!*

Everyone put on their earmuffs,
but not Billy.
"*I love bells!*" he shouted.